The Day and Life of a working Mom!

Michele Linn Griffith

God Is My Rock!

About The Author!

Michele Linn Griffith is a fictional writer, and an avid reader, who lives in Alabama with her family.

mgriffith75@yahoo.com

Philippians 4:13

This story is the product of the authors imagination and all naming of the characters, places, incidents and business are fictitious.

CHAPTER 1

"Mom, why are we moving from our home in New York, where are so close to everything?" asked Levi.

"Son we've been through this, we need a change of scenery," said Doreen.

"Okay, whatever you say mom, but it's not what I want," Levi said huffy. "You know, mom this would be easier if dad was with us."

"Yes son, it would be, but your dad and I aren't together anymore and won't be," Doreen said aggravatedly.

Levy just rolled his eyes, "mumbling whatever."

"Listen son, I know you're mad and hurting because of the difficult changes in our lives but you have to understand, things changed, and people change," Doreen said heartbrokenly.

"Yes mom, I know and understand this, you and dad have me with this information," Levy said nonchalantly. Doreen smiled at her son.

Doreen was in her own thoughts thinking about the last couple of months with her so called husband Ben, who informed her that he wanted a divorce a couple of months back.

They had been married fifteen years which had been tough. Tough didn't cover it, their marriage she thought was built on love and respect for one another, but she found out that it was a total lie on his part. What she was love and respect was not that at all, it was built on lies of all sorts.

Although it took her a few years to figure it out.

With Ben's busy schedule of work and

out of town trips, and not to mention her busy work schedule, and being a mom of a son who is sixteen now. And her son at this moment was missing his dad more than ever, but that never stopped Ben his father from being non-existent in his only son's life, which left her to play both roles, which wasn't easy.

Now she and her son are getting ready to head to the airport to jump on airplane heading to the south which she hasn't been since she moved to Upstate new York at the tender age of eighteen to start her new life with her new husband, and then three short years later their son Levy came into the world, but soon after her world was turned upside down with a newborn and a non-existent husband.

A month later when she was comfortable being a mom, a single mom at that, although she was married but Ben was never home, he was to busy to be to be a husband and father. She to herself that she would be the constant in her son's life, no matter what. Her son was her whole world and she planned to prove it to him.

Doreen was still in her own little world, when she her son calling her name, from somewhere deep inside her head.

After a few minutes she came back to earth, saying "yes son." "Mom the cab is here."

"Okay good," said Doreen, and she and her son quickly grabbed their luggage pieces and then headed out the door.

As they walked up to the cab, the driver opened the door saying "leave your luggage pieces and get inside. Doreen smiled, and then ushered her son into the back of the cab.

A few minutes later, the driver climbed inside and asking, "where to?" "Take us to the airport," said Doreen. "Yes ma'am," he said.

As the cab was pulling away, "hey mom." "Yes son." "Mom tell me again, where are we going?" asked Levy questionably.

"Well son we are moving down south to Mississippi," Doreen said patiently.

"Yea, I know this part mom, I meant, where in Mississippi, are we moving to?" Levy asked.

"Well son, we are moving to Everdeen Mississippi, where Grandma Arlene lives," Doreen said fawnly. Levy smiled, "okay."

The cab pulled up in front of the airport sliding glass doors saying, "we're here, the driver said," as he exited, and slid to the back and started unloading the luggage pieces, while Doreen and her son exited.

The cab driver had their luggage pieces loaded unto a pushcart, as Doreen handed him a cash tip. He smiled, and then walked back to the driver side and climbed into the cab and soon after he was gone. Doreen and her son walked through the doors pulling the pushcarts behind them.

As the doors were sliding shut, Doreen was scanning the area for the nearest check in station, and quickly she spotted the first one and they started heading towards the first station.

As they were walking up, Doreen noticed there were only a couple of people in line and so they hurried into line.

The line was moving fairly quick, and soon it was their turn and the smiling woman, "asked for her license and tickets," which she had purchased online.

A few minutes later an attendant came and collected their pushcart full of luggage pieces, while they were directed to the terminal.

The line moved quickly and then it was their turn to be seated.

Once they were seated and the attendant was out of earshot, "mom." "Yes son." "Mom, how is this flight?" "Well son, I'm not totally sure," said Doreen. "I just know we're on this flight and then we will change flights in Atlanta Georgia."

"Mom." "Yes son." "Mom, I'm curious, what are you going to do for a job in Everdeen Mississippi?" asked Levy curiously.

"I don't know son," she said. "I'll just have to see what kind of jobs are out there and go from there," Doreen said. Levy said, "okay."

"So, son, are you ready to start a new high school?" she asked.

"Yea, I guess, but I really have no choice in the matter, do I," he said.

"No son, I'm afraid not," she said. "Son, I promise everything is going to be alright." "We're going to start our new life in Mississippi with Grandma Arlene."

"Now, how about you lay back and play on your game, while I start my job search." Levy smiled, "sounds good to me."

Doreen quickly sent her mom an email letting her know they were on their way and then pushed send, and then went to the search engine and started her job search.

CHAPTER 2

Arlene was sitting at her computer

when she saw that her email icon was flashing, and so she clicked on it and the email came into view and it was from her daughter Doreen letting her know they were on her way.

She had mixed emotions about her daughter coming back home. She hadn't seen her since left for New York when she was just eighteen. Her baby-girl at that time couldn't wait to leave and be on her own.

Sure, throughout the years her baby girl would come visit but not for long periods of time due to her no-good husband. She could honestly say that she never liked Ben Peterson, he wasn't good enough for her girl, but then again, she never liked any of the boys her daughter brought home. They weren't what she wanted for her only daughter.

Her son David on the other hand had

proved to be the one that had everything together. He had a great job, beautiful wife and sweet daughter.

Doreen her thirty-five year old daughter, was moving back home because of a devastating divorce, but she was glad to have her daughter and grandson back home, but that didn't mean she didn't have mixed emotions about the whole situation.

Her daughter was coming back to the very place that she wanted to run from so long ago because of the loss of her father. He too was a no-good evil man who didn't deserve a decent wife and two great kids.

John Davenport was the man, she thought she could be with him the rest of her life, but she soon figured out that he wasn't the man she needed.

She got rid of him when her kids were at a young age of five and three.

She, being a single mother of two young kids proved to be hard, but really rewarding because, she knew that in the end she would win everything, and John would lose out on everything. So, she worked two job to provide for her kids throughout the years and it was well worth it because her daughter and son were over the top smarter and driven due to her loving raising ways. Both her kids went to college.

Her son went to college to be Lawyer and her and her daughter went to college to be a teacher. In fact, her daughter Doreen was a teacher for fifteen years at a high school in New York which she loved.

Arlene smiled to herself, deep down she was totally excited about her daughter finally coming home, and hopefully she will find her will to live her life for her and her son. She surely deserved it and more.

Arlene glanced at the clock and she noticed it was close to ten at night and it was time for her to get on the road to pick her daughter and grandson up at the airport.

She quickly picked up her keys and the paper with the flight information and it and then headed out the door.

CHAPTER 3

Doreen was proud of herself she had successfully sent out several resumes to several schools for various teaching positions.

She looked over to see her son had fallen asleep playing a game. She smiled. He was her everything.

Where they were moving to school had

already started. It started the at after Labor Day, which was three days ago. He would start first thing Monday morning at Everdeen High School where she had gone.

She looked down at her phone noticing it was after eleven and they would be landing in the next thirty minutes to an hour and of course her mother would be there waiting on them.

It had been a long time since she had been home, of course she and her family had visited throughout the years, but they never stayed long periods of time. Then it hit her she would be walking back into the same home that her father had left them so long ago. The hurt and anger still linger. She didn't know how she would feel seeing her mother for the first time in years.

She was starting to feel so many emotions that it was making her stomach cramp.

She tried to relax and calm her emotions but after a few minutes they were still there. She suddenly heard the attendant announce that they would be landing in the next ten to fifteen minutes.

Her son started stirring, "wake up baby-boy, we're getting read to land in a few minutes," she said. "Okay mom," he said.

The attendants voice came through the microphone saying the plane was getting ready to land, so be seated and then they felt the plane touch down on the tarmac coming to a stop.

Once the plane was stopped, the doors were opening, and everyone was starting to line the aisle.

When it came to be their turn, they

quickly stood up grabbing their belongings and stepping into the aisle following the line of passengers.

They stepped out of the plane and followed the passengers down the long terminal aisle which led into the giant airport.

The line of passengers moved quickly, and soon Doreen was in the airport, she quickly scanned the area for her mom which didn't take long. "Levy I see Grandma Arlene." "Great," he said. "Well come on son," and so they moved through the crowd quickly.

As the crowd thinned, she spotted her mother across the way and they moved towards her.

Arlene was standing waiting patiently when she suddenly spotted her daughter and grandson coming towards her, her nerves then kicked in and her emotions were swirling around but she was happy that her daughter was finally coming home.

Her daughter walked up, "hey mom." Hey baby-girl." "It's been way to long." "Yes mom, it has," Doreen said teary eyed, and both women hugged.

After a few minutes they pulled apart, "wow baby-girl you're so beautiful." "Thanks mom and so are you." Arlene smiled. She looked at Levy, "wow buddy, how handsome are you," and she wrapped her arms around him.

"Levy buddy, it's so good to see you and we're going to have so much fun, I promise son," Arlene said affectionally.

"Well now, how about we go collect your luggage and get out of here," said Arlene, and so they headed over to the luggage claims unit, and soon after Doreen walked up and handed the lady her luggage slip and the lady keyed in the information and then picked up the phone and quietly spoke into the phone, and then she replaced it. "Alright Mrs. Peterson your luggage will be brought out in a few minutes." "Thanks," she said, and then Doreen turned around and ushered her mom and son over to the side.

Within moments the attendant came walking out pushing their pushcart, "here you go Mrs. Peterson," he said. "Thanks," Doreen said, and so they headed through the airport and out the door where her mother's van was waiting, they started climbing inside, while the attendant quickly loaded the trunk.

Within minutes she heard the trunk slam shut, she put the van into drive and started pulling out into traffic. "Well dear, how does it feel to be back in the south?" Arlene asked curiously.

"Oh, I don't know, maybe a little nerve wracking," Doreen said. "Mom, I haven't been back in Mississippi in a very long time, not to mention I have a lot of uneasy memories here."

"Yes dear, I know," said Arlene. "Well maybe, when you get settled in, you find a job and reconnect with some of your old friend, maybe then you'll feel home again."

"Yea maybe, but I don't know though," said Doreen. "Too much time has passed and my friends from way back when, now have their own lives."

"Yea maybe, but dear you'll be surprise there are few of your friends that would love to reconnect with you," Arlene said.

"Alright mom, we will see," Doreen

said. Arlene smiled.

"So, Levy, are you ready to start a new school Monday?" asked Arlene curiously.

"I don't know, maybe grandma," he said. He sighed and then said, "but to be honest I really wish I was back in my old school with my friends."

"Yes son, I know, but things change, and we just have to adjust to the life changes," Arlene said. "Yea whatever," he said.

Arlene shook her head, she understood her grandson's feelings, he's sixteen and having to leave the only home and school he's ever known and all because of the selfish ways of his father, and so therefore here we are.

Doreen pulled into the driveway of her old home, and suddenly all the memories and hard feelings rushed over her, she couldn't help think that she was making a mistake, but then again making mistakes were apart of fixing mistakes that came with life. She took a couple of deep calming breaths and felt herself calming down.

She heard her mom ask, "dear, are you okay?" "Yes mom, I'm okay." "It's just me coming back here for the first time in a very long time."

She drove down the driveway, which looked the same as she left it so long ago, "wow mom this place looks the same, as I left it so long ago."

"Yes dear, I wouldn't change it, it's home," Arlene clarified. "It's your home and always has been." "You and your brother are my world, and that has never changed and never will." Doreen smiled, "thanks mom." "Anytime Dear," Arlene said.

She pulled up to the two-story house where she and her brother grew up.

Despite having no father in the picture, she and her brother still had a wonderful childhood because of their mom.

They exited her mother's van, Doreen stood looking around at the yard and house remembering the good, bad and the insignificant times.

As they were walking up to the stairs, she heard, "mom." "Yea son." "Mom, seriously we're leaving near the ocean."

"Yes son, we are." He smiled, "well mom this could work." Doreen smiled.

Arlene smiled, "good I'm glad you feel that way son, and so Doreen and her son started unloading the van, while Arlene went to open the door.

Within minutes Doreen and Levy walked through the door pulling their carts, and Doreen couldn't believe it her mom left it the same, "wow mom you left the house the same." "Yes dear, I did," Arlene said. "Why wouldn't though?"

"Well now, why don't you and Levy go get settled in, and I'll see you two later in the morning," Arlene said yawning. "Good night Dear," Arlene said, and then they went their separate ways.

CHAPTER 4

Arlene walked into the kitchen around nine finding her daughter sitting at the kitchen table in front of her laptop, "hey dear, what's ya doing?"

"Oh, I'm just checking the status of my work applications," Doreen said.

"Okay, sounds good," Arlene said. "Well, have you heard anything from any of the schools yet?"

"No not yet but it's only Saturday," Doreen said matter of fact. Arlene smiled.

"Well Dear, I feel sure you'll hear something soon."

"Yea, I hope so," Doreen said. "Well now, what do you say, you, Levy and I got out exploring?" Arlene said.

"Okay sounds good," Doreen said. Arlene smiled, "great." "Well come on then let's get moving," and so Doreen stood up and shaking her head okay and heading in the direction of her room.

CHAPTER 5

Thirty minutes later they were walking out the door and soon after climbing into the van.

"Mom." "Yes son." "Mom, where are

we going?”

"Well son, your grandma thinks we need to go out and explore the town of Everdeen," Doreen said.

"Oh great," he said. "So, I promise you it will be fun," said Doreen encouragingly. "Besides this adventure will give you the feel of the town."

Levy just rolled his eyes, "okay whatever."

As they were driving through town, Doreen was seeing her old town and all the feelings and memories started flooding back to her.

A couple of hours later Arlene pulled back into her driveway, "well son, what do you think?"

"Um, it'll do, I guess," he said. Arlene smiled, "okay I'll take that."

"Well grandma I'm going to go and checkout the beach now, he said."

"Alright, son just stay close, and have fun," Arlene said.

He smiled, "yes ma'am," and then he went to his room to change.

Within minutes he came rushing back down the stairs and out the door with towel in hand.

He walked down the steps and onto the sandy path, the breeze hit him gently.

He walked down the path down to the open beach which was littered with people scattered all over.

He quickly found himself a place to sit, and he laid out his towel and then sat down letting the hot sun hit him.

He'd never really been to a beach in his life. His family always went to the mountains or state parks, or waterparks.

He was sitting there enjoying the sun and the sand and the peacefulness of the beach when suddenly someone walked up saying, "hi." He looked up seeing a boy about his age, "hi."

"What's your name?" the boy asked curiously.

"I'm Levy," Levy said. "Well nice to meet you Levy, and I'm Seth." "Hi Seth," Levy said shyly.

"You must be new, because I've never seen you around here before," said Seth.

"Yea, I just moved here," said Levy. "Oh okay, well when did you get here?" asked Seth.

"Uh, early this morning," said Levy. "Oh wow, so your real new here," said Seth.

Seth smiled. "Well come on, come meet my friends."

"Okay, yea sure," said Levy, and so he

stood up, dusted himself off and then followed Seth over to the group of kids.

They walked up to the group of kids, and Seth called out, "hey everyone this is Levy and he's new here." Seth pointed at the first boy, this is Collin, and then he pointed to the second kid, this is Kate, and then he pointed to the next one, this is Joana, and then he went to the next, this is Jade, and then he went to the next one, this is Niko, and then he pointed to the next, this is Trey, and then he pointed to the next one, this is Yardley." Levy smiled, "hi everyone," and then they sat down.

"So, Levy, where are you from?" asked Levy.

"I'm from Upstate New York," Levy said.

"Wow, you're along way from home," said Seth. "I bet you miss it."

"Yea, I'm a long way from home, and yes I miss it," said Levy.

"So, why did you move here anyway?" asked Seth curiously.

"My mom's decision to move here," he said matter of fact.

"Oh okay, sorry man about that," said Seth. "Man, we know all about them crazy parent choices."

"So, who did you move with anyway?" asked Seth.

"Me and my mom moved here," said Levy. "We're living with grandma for right now."

"Okay, that's cool," said Seth. "So, I take it you're in the tenth grade, right?"

"Yes, I'm in the ten grade," said Levy. "Back in my old school, I was an honor student."

"Oh yea," said Seth cautiously. "So, do

you like or play sports?”

“Yes, I like sports,” said Levy. “I play hockey, baseball, soccer, and basketball.”

“Oh good, that’s cool,” said Seth. “Well come on let’s go get in the ocean.”

Levy smiled, “alright,” and then the group ran towards the ocean.

CHAPTER 6

Arlene was sitting on the porch looking out at the ocean when she heard the sliding glass door slid open and then slid shut, and then her daughter sat down beside her, “where’s Levy?”

“He said he was going to the beach for a while,” Arlene said.

“Okay, well I’m hoping he’s having fun,” said Doreen.

Arlene smiled, “I hope he’s having fun

too." "Maybe he'll meet friends."

"Yea, I hope so and soon," Doreen said. "Mom he's been through so much, that he needs someone or something good in his life."

Arlene shook her head in agreement. The two women sat looking at the ocean and talking catching up.

Levy and his new friends were throwing a football around.

"He man, you're pretty good at throwing a football," said Niko. "Do you play football?"

Levy smiled, "yea a little with friends, not with a team or anything."

"Oh okay, well that's too bad," said Niko. "Well anyway our football team is getting ready to start tryouts Monday if you're interested."

"Yea maybe, but I don't know though," said Seth.

"Alright, well if you're interested just let me know," Niko said. "Well anyway I need to be going," and so Niko went and grabbed his things and started walking away.

Soon after one by one the others started leaving.

When it was just Seth and Levy left, "well man it was nice hanging out with you Levy," said Seth. "Yea, and it was nice meeting you too," said Levy, and then they went and grabbed their things and then headed towards their homes.

Levy was walking up the sandy path, he was happy and grateful for meeting some new people today on the beach.

He was nearing the bottom of his steps

when he heard, "hey man wait for me," and so he turned around seeing Seth running up the path.

"Hey Seth, what are you doing?" asked Levy.

"Well man, I got half-way to my jeep and decided that I wanted to hangout some more with you, if that's okay," said Seth.

"Okay, that's cool," Levy said. Seth smiled, and then they headed up the steps.

"Hey mom, and grandma, this is Seth," Levy said. "We're going to hangout here, if that's okay." Doreen and Arlene smiled.

"Hey Seth, it's nice too meet you," both ladies said. "

"Nice to meet you too," he said, and then they headed inside.

CHAPTER 7

It's six o'clock and its dinner time, and Doreen called, "Levy and Seth dinner is ready."

Within minutes the two boys came walking into the kitchen, "alright boys have a seat." "Yes ma'am," said both, and they sat down.

Doreen and Arlene brought in the plates and set them down on the table, "thanks ma'am for letting me stay for dinner," said Seth.

"Yea sure, and you're more then welcome," they said. "Well now, let's say grace."

An hour and half later dinner was over, while Doreen and Arlene were cleaning up, the boys went back outside.

"Hey man, let's throw the football around," Seth said.

"Yea sure," said Levy, and then they picked up the ball and started throwing it around.

"Wow man, Niko is right you're good at throwing a football, you should tryout Monday for football," Seth said.

"Okay maybe, but I'm not sure yet," said Levy.

Seth smiled, "okay man." "Well anyway I need to be going, but if you want to hangout tomorrow just holler at me "You can find me on facebook under Seth Brooks."

"Okay, I'll hit you up on facebook later man," Levy said, and then Seth started walking away.

Levy walked back up the on the porch finding his mom and Arlene, "well now Seth seems nice," said Doreen.

"Yea he is," said Levy, and then he

went quiet.

"Son, what's wrong?" asked Arlene curiously.

"Well mom and grandma, I met Seth and his friends today and we threw the football around today, and one of the guys thinks I'm good enough to tryout for football on Monday," said Levy.

"Oh yea, well if you want to tryout for football, I say tryout Monday," said Arlene.

"Baby-boy if you want to tryout for football, I say go for it," said Doreen.

Levy smiled, "thanks mom and grandma." "Well I'm going to my room now."

"Okay son, good night, see you tomorrow," they said, and then he headed up the stairs.

He walked into his new room, sat down at the desk and woke up his computer, he first went to his facebook page and looked up Seth Brooks and sent him a friend request, and then he went to his email, found his dads name and then started typing out his lengthy message.

Levy was close enough to his dad, even though he and his mom weren't together anymore.

Thirty minutes went by and he had finished his message and pushed send. He then went back to his facebook page, and saw that Seth had accepted his friend request, and then he sent him a private message with his phone number and then pushed send, and then he exited facebook and then computer, he then turned on his tv and started playing his game.

He'd been playing his game an hour

when he noticed his screen had a flashing icon, and so he stopped his game, and picked up his phone and looked at the screen noticing his email icon was flashing and so he clicked on it, and the email was from his dad and so he started reading it.

When he was finished, he smiled, he was thankful that his dad wanted to be involved with him and everything he was interested in. Even though his mother says otherwise, and that's why he kept this from his mom, he didn't think she would approve.

His mom and dad had been married for as long as he could remember but not happily.

He emailed back saying thank you for

supporting me, dad in everything I want to do and then he pressed send. Suddenly his phone dinged, he quickly picked it up and looked at the screen and saw a message from an unknown number saying hi.

He typed back hi and pushed send. Not long after he received a message saying hi this is Seth.

He messaged back saying hi Seth, what's up?"

For the rest of the night they messaged back and forth while Levy played his game.

CHAPTER 8

Sunday morning rolled around, and it's nine o'clock and Doreen was sitting at the table in front of her computer, when she heard, "good morning dear."

"Oh, good morning mom." "So, what's ya doing dear?" asked Arlene.

"I'm just checking my application status," Doreen said.

"Oh okay, well good luck dear," Arlene said.

"Anyway dear, we need to take Levy school shopping for his new school," said Arlene.

"Okay, yea and you're right," said Doreen, and so she stood up and walked over and called out, "Levy get up and come down son."

Several minutes went by and no Levy, and so she called out again, "Levy son, come on down." She hurried to her room to get dressed.

Levy sat up, and then stood up and went and climbed in the shower.

Several minutes went by and then he exited the shower, toweling off and then he walked back into his room and quickly dressed.

He walked into the kitchen finding his grandma sitting at the table drinking coffee, "good morning grandma."

"Good morning son," she said. "Well now, we have a lot to do today."

"Oh yea, like what?" he asked. "Well son, we're going shopping for your school clothes, shoes and school supplies," she said.

"Oh great, that sounds like so much fun," he said. "Can I at least ask Seth to go with me?"

Arlene smiled, "yea sure." Levy smiled, "thanks." "Well son, you need to call and see if he can go?"

"Yes ma'am," and then he pulled out

his phone and then texted his friend asking him he wanted to go with him today and then pressed send.

Not long after he received a text message from Seth saying yes and I'll be there in a few minutes. He replied back saying okay.

Within minutes they heard a vehicle pull up, and Levy ran out the door, "hey man."

"Hey Levy." "Hey man, see if you can ride with me," said Seth.

"Yea sure, just let me go ask?" said Levy, and then he hurried back inside. "Hey grandma, can I ride with Seth?"

"Yea sure, I don't see any problem with it," said Arlene.

Levy smiled, "thanks grandma." "You're welcome son, and don't worry I'll let your mom know," said Arlene.

"Okay, thanks," and then he ran out the door, and down the steps and then he climbed into the jeep, "well come on let's go," and so Seth started the engine and soon after they were leaving the driveway.

Doreen walked into the kitchen finding Arlene sitting and drinking coffee, "hey mom I'm ready to go." "Has Levy come down yet?"

"Yes, Levy came down, and I gave him permission to ride with Seth," Arlene said.

"Alright, well that's good, I'm glad he has someone new in his life to hangout with, I just wished he'd asked me," said Doreen.

"Yea, well you weren't down here, and so I gave him permission, I didn't think you'd mind," said Arlene. Doreen smiled.

"Well anyway, come on let's get

moving we have a lot to do today," Arlene said, and so they grabbed their things and then headed out the door.

They climbed into the van and soon after they were leaving the driveway.

Seth was driving down the road, "so, what do you think so far?" "I don't know, what do you mean?" asked Levy.

"Well first, have you ever been aloud to ride with anyone your age?" asked Seth.

"No, not really," said Levy. "Although we really didn't drive all that much."

Seth smiled, "okay." "Well now, you have, so what do you think?"

"It's cool, so far," said Levy. "Good," said Seth.

"Now let's go find you some school clothes, shoes and school supplies," said Seth. Levy smiled, "yea I'm game.

Seth pulled into the Everdeen Mall, and quickly parked, and soon after they were walking towards the front entrance.

As they were entering the mall, when Levy's phone buzzed, he looked at his phone screen and saw that it was his mother asking if he was okay and where he was. He replied back saying, yes I'm okay and we are just walking inside and then pressed send.

"So, Levy, where do you want to start?" asked Seth.

"I don't know, I'm not used to being on my own," said Levy.

"Okay, well in that case just follow my lead," Seth said. Levy smiled, "okay."

For the next several hours the boys had fun walking through the mall and shopping for school stuff.

"Wow, we actually found everything I need and more," Levy said.

Seth smiled, "yea, we did, and it was actually fun, and thank you for hanging out with me."

"You're welcome, and it was fun, and I enjoyed every minute of hanging out with you, new kid," said Seth. "Well now, how about we get some food?"

"Yea, that sounds good," said Levy. "So, where are we going?" "I know the perfect place," said Seth.

Levy smiled, "okay, I'm game." Seth smiled.

A few minutes later Seth pulled into Chandlar's Pizza Parlor, "this is the best place for us kids to hangout," Seth said.

Levy smiled, "cool," and then they stepped out and headed inside where they found their other friends and heading over and sat down.

CHAPTER 9

It was around ten o'clock when Seth pulled up in the driveway, and Levy quickly stepped out saying, "bye and see you tomorrow," and then he shut the door, and then he headed up the stairs, as Seth was leaving the driveway.

He walked through the door, "mom and grandma I'm home."

They walked around the corner, "hey son, did you have fun?" they asked.

"Yes ma'am, I did," he said. They smiled, "good we're glad." "Well now, you have school tomorrow."

"Yes ma'am, good night mom and grandma, see you in the morning," he said, and then he headed upstairs.

CHAPTER 10

Monday morning rolled around, and Doreen was in the kitchen drinking coffee and looking on her computer.

By seven o'clock Levy was walking was walking into the kitchen, "good morning mom."

"Oh, good morning son." "So, are you ready for your first day of school at Everdeen?" asked Doreen.

"Yes ma'am," he said. Doreen smiled, "good."

"Mom." "Yea Son." "Mom, Seth is picking me up this morning." "Alright Son," she said.

Around seven fifteen they heard a horn blow, "bye mom, see you later," and then he was out the door.

He climbed into Seth's jeep, "hey man, are you ready for your first day?"

"Yes, I'm ready, as I ever will be," said Levy.

"So, are you going to tryout for our football team?" asked Seth curiously.

"Maybe, but I'm really sure yet," said Levy.

"Alright, whatever you want to do man," Seth said supportively. "Well anyway, let's get to school."

Ten minutes later Seth pulled into the parking lot of Everdeen High School, "well we're here man." "So, are you ready?"

"Yea and no," said Levy. Seth smiled, "come on let's get your schedule and get this day started," and so they climbed out of the jeep and they headed for the front entrance.

Within minutes they were walking through the doors, and into the office, and up to the desk where a woman stood, "yes may I help young man?"

"Yes ma'am, I'm Levy Matthew Peterson, and I'm new here."

"Alright, give me a minute," and tapped a few keys, and soon she found his information, and soon after she was handing him a paper, "here you go, here's your schedule, and a map of the school and few other things," she said.

"Thanks ma'am," he said. "You're welcome and welcome to Everdeen High School," she said. He smiled.

"Now, Seth you'll be Levy's escort for today," she said. "Yes ma'am, he said.

"Well come on Levy let's get started," and so they headed out of the office.

They stopped, and Seth scanned Levy's schedule noticing that Levy had all his classes, "well man it looks like we've got all the same classes so just follow my lead," and so they headed down the hall.

CHAPTER 11

Ben was sitting at his desk, his thoughts were on his son Levy. He missed his son something terrible.

It was nice to receive an email from him last night letting him know that they had made it to Everdeen Mississippi, but he wasn't happy about it either.

He didn't understand why Doreen had decided to move out of state so quick, it didn't make sense, but on the other hand nothing ever made sense with her, or maybe it was just him.

They had tried to make their relationship work a couple of times, but it was a struggle. It was partly his fault, and partly hers and party their families.

His thoughts traveled back to his son Levy and everything he's going through. But the one thing he could say about his son was that he was extremely smart and good at everything he does, and at that moment it hit him that he needed to make a trip down to Everdeen Mississippi and soon to see his son.

The more he thought about his up and coming trip, the more he realized it needed to happen soon.

CHAPTER 12

Doreen was sitting at the kitchen table in front of her computer reading the email that she'd received.

She was so happy and relieved that the Everdeen Elementary School had emailed her letting her know she was selected to be interviewed that afternoon, and so she replied back saying I accept the invitation of the interview for this afternoon, and then she pushed send.

She was smiling to herself, when Arlene walked into the kitchen, "good morning dear." What's ya doing?"

"Oh, good morning mom." "And I'm reading an email from Everdeen Elementary School letting me know that I've been selected for an interview this afternoon," she said excitedly.

"Oh wow, that's awesome dear and congratulations," Arlene said happily.

"Well, I need to get a shower and get ready," Doreen said, and then she stood up and headed out of the room.

Arlene just stood their smiling to herself she was happy for daughter.

Her daughter had been through a lot in the past couple of months and she felt bad for her.

She just hoped that this job worked out for her daughter and soon.

CHAPTER 13

Ben was sitting at his desk in front of his computer, he couldn't help thinking about his son and his ex-wife.

It bothered him that Doreen had just up and left the state and all because he wanted a divorce from her.

Although now he's kicking himself for his crazy decision of divorce back a couple of months ago.

The more he thought about everything, the more he realized he needed to reach out to his son, and at that moment he decided to send his son an email.

CHAPTER 14

Three o'clock rolled around, and Levy and Seth walked out of their last class, "so, what do you think so far?" asked Seth curiously.

"I don't know," said Levy. It was alright." "But it's nothing like my old school," said Levy. "In fact, the classes that I went through today are review for me."

"Oh yea," said Seth. "Well that's crazy, your school must be really far ahead."

"Yea, something like that," said Levy. "Uh huh." "Well alrighty then," said Seth.

"So, Levy, have you thought anymore

about the football tryouts?" asked Seth curiously.

"Yea, and I think I want to tryout," said Levy.

Seth smiled, "alrighty then, let's go," and they headed out the door.

Not long after they walked up to Seth's jeep and climbed inside. Levy pulled out his phone and sent his mom a message letting her know that he was going football tryouts and then he pressed send.

A few minutes later he received a message from his mom saying okay and good luck buddy. He texted back saying thank you mom and then he pressed send.

Seth pulled into the parking lot of the Everdeen Green-Devils football stadium and found a parking space and soon after they we're walking towards the field.

They walked inside the field and up to a group of guys, where the coach was just getting ready to talk to the team, when the coach looked saying, "hi Seth." "Who do you have with you?"

"Hi coach Webster, and this is Levy Peterson, who is new here," Seth said.

"Well, welcome Levy to Everdeen High School," said Coach Webster." "Well then, Levy have you ever played football before?"

"Yea, but not on an actually team," said Levy.

"Okay, well then, let's see what can do," said Coach. Coach Webster looked up looking at his potential team and saying, "everyone this is Levy and he's new here," and so the group of boys walked over and introduced themselves to Levy.

After a few minutes, Coach Webster called, "hey everyone let's get started."

CHAPTER 14

Doreen was sitting at the kitchen table in front of her computer reading through her email when she came across one from Ben her ex-husband, and she decided to leave that for later, she was to happy and excited about her new job which she was starting tomorrow at the Everdeen Elementary School, to ruin with an email from him. But she couldn't help wonder, what he could possibly want? He made it clear to her that a divorce is what he wanted, that he could do a lot better than her.

Her thoughts traveled to her son Levy, she was hoping that his first day of school was good, and that football tryouts were going good for him. All she ever wanted was her son to have the very best of everything. After all he was her everything.

She looked at the time seeing that it was nearing six o'clock, she decided to go ahead and read her ex-husband's email, and so she clicked on it and started reading.

Several minutes went by and she finished reading the email, and she sat there staring into space. She couldn't believe it, he was actually apologizing to her for everything. She didn't know how to react to that, or even how to feel.

He really didn't give her any kind of reasoning for their breakup divorce, it was just what he wanted. But he never asked her what she wanted. In, fact their whole relationship and marriage were about him solely. He never asked her for or about anything, and that drove her crazy.

The more she thought about his email and he, the more she realized she needed to email him back laying everything out and so she started her email.

She was so engrossed in her email that she didn't hear the front door open or shut until her son sat down beside her saying, "hey mom." She looked over, "hey son."

"So, how was your first day of school son?"

"It was okay," he said. "Mom, I'm so far ahead of them, that its not even funny."

"Oh no, sorry son," she said. "So, what do you want to do?"

"Mom, I don't know right now," he said. "I guess, I'm just going to go through this week and see how it goes."

"Okay son, whatever you want to do," she said. "So, how did football tryouts go tonight?"

"Um, they went good, I think," he said. "I should know something tomorrow."

She smiled, "good." "Son, I'm so proud of you." "Thanks mom," he said smiling.

"So, what you mom, how was your day?" he asked curiously.

"Actually son, my day was good, I start a new job tomorrow at Everdeen Elementary," she said excitedly.

"Well mom, I'm going to my room to work on some homework," he said.

"Okay son, good night, see you in the morning," she said, and he stood up and walked over to the counter grabbing a couple of snacks and something to drink on his way out of the room.

When he was out of sight, she just smiled and shaking her head happily. Her son was her greatest accomplishment.

He was so smart, talented and dedicated in every aspect of his life, that she couldn't ask for a better kid.

Levy was up in his room working on the homework from his classes, which was easy. He was used to challenging work, and this to him was anything but.

He noticed his email icon was flashing, and so he clicked on it and he saw that the email was from his father, and so he started reading it.

The email was relatively short and to the point. He and his father were close but not close enough to hangout in the same place or state for very long.

His father was more of the monetary father who made sure he had everything he needed or wanted but that happened behind his mothers back because his father didn't want her knowing anything about his help towards him. He used to tell me it was our little secret.

The more he thought about his father and his unique ways, the more he realized he needed to reach out his father because it seemed that his father needed him at this point, and he actually felt bad for him, because he really had no one, and so he started typing out his message.

CHAPTER 15

Tuesday morning rolled around, and Doreen was in her room getting ready for her new job as a kindergarten teacher at Everdeen Elementary School, and she was so excited.

Levy was in his room getting ready for his second day of school, but he couldn't help but think about his father's email. It was bothering him. He would have a sit down with his father when he got here in the next couple of days, he would make sure of it.

He grabbed his things, and then headed down the stairs and into the kitchen finding his grandma sitting at the kitchen table drinking her coffee, "hey grandma."

"Good morning son." "Are you ready for your second day of school?"

"Yea, I guess," he said. "I really have no choice in the matter, do I?"

She smiled, "no son, I'm afraid not." He smirked, "I figured." Suddenly they heard a horn blow, "bye grandma, love you, see you later tonight," and then he was walking out the door.

He walked down the stairs and over to the jeep and climbed in, "hey buddy." "Hey Seth."

"So, Levy, did you finish the homework last night?" asked Seth.

"Yea, of course I finished the lame homework, why wouldn't I?" Levy said.

Seth smiled, "yea, me too." "I understand where you're coming from." "The classes are lame, but it's school, and we have to attend them to get enough credits to graduate."

He went to his own thoughts, thinking about the extra credit programs that the counselor had told him about, and he was seriously thinking about checking into them. They sounded interesting. He would go online and search them out.

Doreen walked into the Everdeen

Elementary School, and into the office, the women behind the desk asked, "yes ma'am, may I help you?"

"Yes ma'am, I'm Ms. Doreen Peterson, and I'm the new Kindergarten teacher."

"Oh, yes ma'am, welcome." "Just a minute."

A couple of minutes later a man came walking out, "hi Ms. Peterson, I'm Mr. Hesterly and I'm the principle, please follow me to your new class."

Doreen smiled, "yes sir," and then she followed him out the door.

CHAPTER 16

Ben was sitting at his desk, he'd just finished setting up his plane information for the weekend. He was happy and excited about seeing his son, and maybe his ex-wife, but more so he needed this small vacation.

His job was way more stressful then anything that he ever thought could be.

Being a lawyer was such a big responsibility and very stressful, especially with the ever so many people needing lawyers for just about everything known to man. Especially in New York city.

He thought back to when it all started. He was seventeen when he graduated high school with honors, and then soon after he went to college at the University of Berkeley where he finished top of his class.

He and Doreen married right after high school, and soon after they found out they were pregnant with Levy, but him being college and trying to work full time and being married didn't work as well as he wanted it to, or thought it would.

He didn't realize just how hard it would be. But they tried over the years to make things work because of Levy, up until a couple months ago, and he found himself seeing another woman, which really wasn't Doreen's fault, it was his.

Doreen really didn't do anything wrong. It was all him. He was all business, all the time, and nothing else. Where, as she was the mother, protector, supporter, provider and everything in between, that he couldn't do.

He hated himself for everything that he couldn't, or didn't do for her, or their son or their family. Unlike him, she put their son first and foremost, and she did what she had to do for him and herself.

He was hoping and praying that this visit this weekend would help heal him, and Doreen and their son Levy, but more so he's hoping to restore some kind of friendship, between himself and Doreen, but they would see. He smiled to himself.

CHAPTER 17

Levy was sitting at lunch by himself at the moment, he was looking at his phone reading about the online extra credit work, which peeked his interested. It peeked his interested so much that he sent an email requesting information and then pushed send. He then went back to searching on the web for whatever peeked, his interest. Although he loved taking pictures and drawing, he just wasn't sure which one he liked more. He even wasn't sure what profession he wanted to go for at this moment. He had many choices he just wasn't sure which one peeked, his interest the most. Suddenly he was interrupted by the chatter of other students invading his privacy, and so he stood up grabbing his things and walking away.

CHAPTER 18

Three o'clock rolled around, and Levy and Seth were walking out of their last class, "hey man, was today better?"

"Yea, today was a little better," Levy said.

Seth smiled, "good." "Now, let's go find out if we've made the team or not."

Levy smiled, "yes let's, I'm ready," and so they headed out the door.

Seth pulled into the parking lot of the football stadium, "hey man let's go change before we go to the field." "Yea sure," said

Levy.

They hurried out of the jeep and over to the locker room.

Within minutes they came out of the locker room heading towards the field.

They walked into the field where coach was getting ready to address the group, "welcome possible team." "Now, as you well know we are looking for new team members to join our Green-Devil team, and I've got couple of names written down but I need names, so let me see what you guys got, so lets get started."

Doreen was walking out the door, she was happy but extremely tired. Her first day of school kicked her butt. Those kindergarteners were something serious. But she loved her job, it was rewarding and fun.

She walked up to her car, and climbed inside, and soon after she was leaving the parking lot.

She pulled into her driveway ten minutes later, and soon after she was walking towards the steps.

She walked onto the porch finding her mom sitting on the swing, "hey mom." "Hey dear." "So, how was your first day today?"

"My day was awesome," she said. "The school is small, but the teachers are nice and helpful."

"Mom, I forgot how different Mississippi schools are from New York, but I like the smallness of towns and I'm glad to be back home." "Well now, I'm going to go get changed," said Doreen, and then she headed inside heading towards her room, all the while thinking about her ex-husband's last email, and she's hoping that she read it wrong, but she didn't think she did, and so that meant that this weekend they could possibly could have a visitor.

The more she thought about her ex-husband and his possible visit, the more it made her uneasy. The thought of seeing him made her uneasy. She wasn't sure about herself. She wasn't sure if her feelings for him would come flooding back.

Her thoughts immediately traveled to her son, she didn't know how he would feel about seeing his father, and a that moment she decided she would sit down and talk to her son when he got home.

CHAPTER 19

Seven thirty and football tryouts were

over, and Coach Webster was looking over his paperwork, and looked up saying, "alright guys, I have the lineup for this seasons up and coming roster, so come over and take a look," he said, and so the group of guys headed over.

Levy and Seth were walking back to the jeep, "omg we actually made it onto the roster," said Seth happily.

Levy smiled, "yea we did, and it feels good."

Not long after the guys were climbing into the jeep, and soon after Seth was leaving the parking lot.

He pulled into the driveway, and Levy climbed out saying, "thanks man, see you tomorrow."

"Yea, man, see you tomorrow, and you're welcome," said Seth, and then he was leaving.

Levy walked into the house, "hey mom and grandma, I'm home."

Within minutes they came walking into the room, "hey son, how was your day?"

"It was good," he said. "In, fact I made the football roster."

"That's awesome son, and congratulations," they said happily.

"Mom." "Yes son." "Mom, I'm looking into some extra credit classes, is that alright with?" he asked.

"Yes sure, son," she said. "So, son, are they related to high school or what?" she asked curiously.

"Um, well mom they're actually college course credits," he said matter of fact." "Mom, I'm so far ahead of this school that I'm bored." "Bored to the point of going further in the studies ahead of everyone."

"Alright son, and I understand, and I was afraid of this, so I'm going to say yes to you going through with the extra college courses."

Levy smiled, "thanks mom." "And to be honest, I've already started."

She smiled, "yea, I figured you had." "Now son, I have something I need to talk to you about."

"Alright, what?" he asked cautiously. "Well son, it has to do with your father," she said.

"Um, okay, what about him?" Levy asked. Although he had a feeling that she was going to tell him that his father wants to reconnect with him and soon, but he didn't know his feelings on that right now. Even though he and his father had a relationship, but it wasn't built on love or respect, but strictly monetarily.

He never really knew his father on any other level, but what on a monetarily level, but then again it would be nice maybe to get to know the man who helped give him. life.

"Well son, I think your father is making plans to visit and soon, and I just wanted you to know." "So, what are your feelings on this?"

"Mom, I don't know," he said. "I really don't know the man to be honest." Although it would be cool to see my father and get to know him as a person, and not just as the man who gives me money, when I ask for it." Suddenly he realized what he'd said, "oh no, did I just say that out loud?"

"Yes son, you did." Although she already knew about Ben and Levy's agreement with the monetary responsibility of Ben. She overheard them discussing it way back when Levy was just little boy. Ben didn't want to be apart of Levy's life, but he didn't want to be cut out totally either, so that's how the monetary relationship came about.

"Levy smiled, "thanks mom." "But I hate to tell you this whether you like it or not, this is how father and I deal with each other. Although secretly he's always wanted more from his father, and maybe now he and his father and have an actual relationship between them.

"Mom, it's fine with me if he comes to visit," he said.

She smiled, "okay son, I'll let him know."

"Well anyway, I'm going to my room now, good night son," and then he headed out of the room.

He walked into his room, dropped his bag and then he sat down at his desk, woke up his computer and went to his email and started typing out his message to his father.

CHAPTER 20

Friday afternoon rolled around, and Ben was walking out of his office heading towards the exit, all the while thinking about the crazy last couple of working at work, and his vacation that was starting now and he was so happy.

Within several strides he walked up to his suv, and quickly putting his stuff in the back seat, and then afterwards he climbed inside, started his engine, and soon after he was heading out of the parking lot.

As he was driving down the road, he was happy and relieved that he was going on a much-needed vacation. It had been years sense he'd been anywhere on vacation. Come to think of it, he'd never really taken any kind of time off work in eighteen years.

He hadn't back in Mississippi sense he'd been seventeen years old. He left right after graduation heading to New York and never looked back.

He turned the radio on and let the music seep in and wash over him.

Doreen was finishing up with the straightening of her classroom when her phone started buzzing, she stopped what she was doing, and pulled out her phone out of her pocket, and she looked at her screen seeing that the message was from Ben saying he was on his way to the airport.

She messaged him back saying okay,

see you soon and then she pressed send. She then shoved her phone back in her pocket and then she went back to what she was doing, all the while thinking about the arrival of her ex-husband sometime tonight.

Ben pulled into the parking lot of the Metro-Deason Airport, and quickly found a parking spot.

Within minutes he was walking towards the front entrance.

He walked through the sliding glass doors and straight up to the counter, "yes sir, how may I help you?"

"Yes ma'am, here's my flight information," he said.

"Yes sir," and she tapped a few keys and then said, alright here you are, you're all set," and so she handed him the paperwork and the pointed him in the direction of terminal D, and so he grabbed his pushcart and headed down the crowded airport.

Within minutes he walked up to the line of terminal D.

The line moved quickly and before he knew it, it was his turn, and so he handed the lady the paperwork, and she tapped a few keys and then said, "here you go sir," and she handed him paperwork, and said, "alright you can enter the terminal aisle," and so he walked through the door and down the aisle.

He walked up to the plane entrance where he was met by a stewardess saying, "welcome Mr. Peterson, come follow me," and so he followed her down the tight aisle about halfway and she pointed to his seat and then she headed back to the front.

He placed his luggage pieces in the overhead compartment, and then placed his computer bag and briefcase in the seat next to him, and then he sat down, pulling out his phone and text messaging Doreen letting her know that he was on the airplane.

Doreen was walking through the door when het phone buzzed, she pulled it out and saw that the message was from Ben letting her know he was on the airplane. She text messaged back saying see you in a couple of hours and then she pressed send.
She hurried through the house, and into her room and quickly changed and then went to work on cleaning and straightening up the house.

CHAPTER 21

It was six thirty and Doreen and Arlene had dinner nearly finished when her phone buzzed, she pulled out her phone and looked at the screen seeing it was from Levy saying he was on his way home. She texted back okay good, your father will be here any minute and then she pressed send.

"Well now, take it that was Levy," said Arlene.

"Yes ma'am, that was Levy, and he's on his way home," said Doreen.

Arlene smiled, "so my girl, are you ready for this visit from Ben?" asked Arlene curiously.

"I don't know mom," she said. "All I know is that this is going to be one interesting weekend."

Arlene smiled, "yea, no doubt dear." "This is going to be an interesting weekend, to say the least." "Well anyway, we'll just go with it."

"So, dear what does Levy think about his father coming for a visit this weekend?"

"He seems to be okay with it, when asked him about it earlier?" Doreen said.

Seth pulled into the driveway, and Levy stepped out, "well man, I'll see you sometime this weekend," said Levy, and then he headed towards the stairs, as Seth backed out of the driveway.

Levy walked through the door, "hey mom and grandma, I'm home."

He walked into the kitchen, "hey mom, and grandma."

"Hey buddy," they said. "How was your day today?"

"It was good, I'm incorporating regular school courses and college courses together, so it's going better now, and not so boring," he said.

"Good, I'm glad you're finding a way to deal with this new school and getting ahead, she said." "I'm so proud of you son."

"So, son, are you excited about seeing your father?" she asked curiously.

"Yea, I guess mom," he said. "All though I really don't know him, it'd be nice to get to know him as my dad and nothing more," he said.

"So, when will he be here anyway?" asked Levy curiously.

"Well son, he should be here soon," said Doreen.

"Aright." "Well, do I have time to go get a shower and change?" he asked.

"Yea sure, go get yourself a shower and a change of clothes, I'll let you know when he gets here," she said, and so he smiled, and then headed up the stairs.

CHAPTER 22

Seven thirty rolled around, and Levy came rushing down, when a knock sounded at the door, and so he rushed down the rest of the stairs and over to the door and he opened it finding his father standing in the doorframe, "dad."

"Hey son." "Well it's good to see you son," Ben said.

"Yea, and it's good to see you dad," Levy said. "Well come on in, and welcome," and so Ben walked through the door, and then quickly Levy shut it back. "Well come on let's go into the kitchen," and so they hurried through the house and walked into the kitchen finding Doreen and Arlene loading the table with food, "mom, look who's here." Doreen and Arlene looked up, "oh good, you're here Ben, come sit down."

"Thanks," he said. "Wow, everything looks and smells good."

"Thanks," they said. "So, Ben how was your flight?" Doreen asked.

"It was good," he said. "That's good, good to hear," said Doreen.

"Well now, Levy, why don't you tell me something about yourself?" Ben said.

"Well, what d you want to know?" asked Levy.

"Anything." "Everything," he said. "Alright, well let's see, I'm a sophomore." "I'm an honor student who loves painting, drawing and photographing everything." "And now I'm on a football team in a new school and town." "And, oh yeah, I just started taking online college courses for extra credits."

"Oh wow, that's awesome son, and it

sounds like you're doing great with everything," said Ben.

"Thanks dad," he said. "Dad, I'm not going to lie to you this move was really nerve wracking, and to be honest I really didn't want to move from New York but we had to, we didn't have a choice in the matter." "We've been here a week, and I have a couple of friends already."

Ben smiled, "wow son, I'm sorry that you've had to uproot your life, but I promise it will be a good change." "A slower pace."

"So, dad, tell me something about you," said Levy.

"Well son, what do you want to know?" Ben asked.

"Um, well first, how long have you been a lawyer?" "Secondly, how did you get started?" "Next, what made you want to be a lawyer?" "Next, do you like sports?" "If so, which ones?" "Do you have hobbies?" "What are they?"

"Alright, well to answer your first question, I was twenty-two when I became a lawyer."

"I've always liked the criminal justice, it's always been intriguing to me, so I put in several applications and resumes to various companies and soon after Miller, Thomas and Gumus, offered me a very decent job offer, one I couldn't refuse."

"I love sports, and always have," said Ben. "I really don't have a favorite sport, they all appeal to me."

"I have a few hobbies, I love to draw, paint and photograph anything and everything."

"Son, do you have any more questions for me?" asked Ben curiously.

"Yes, how long are you staying? asked Levy.

"Um, well I'm planning on staying through Sunday day," he said.

"Oh okay, cool then," said Levy. "So, what do we have planned for, for tomorrow?"

"I don't know yet son, whatever you want to do," said Ben.

Levy smiled, "alright, I'll be thinking about it, mom I'm going to my room now."

"Okay, son, see you tomorrow," Doreen said.

"Nice seeing you dad, good night," said Levy.

"Yea, nice seeing you son, and good night," said Ben.

"Good night, grandma, see you in the morning," said Levy, and then he stood up and headed for the stairs.

When Levy was out of sight, "alright Ben, tell me, why you are really here?" said Doreen.

"Okay, that's my que," said Arlene. "Good night, and I'll see you in the morning," and so she stood up and headed out of the room.

When Arlene was out of sight, "alright now, tell me Ben, why are you really here?" Doreen said forcefully.

He sat their quietly, contemplating on what to tell her. He didn't know exactly where to start.

He took a couple of deep calming breaths, and then said, "Doreen we go way back to childhood."

"Yea, we do," she said. "So, why are you here Ben?"

"Doreen, I'm here to see you and my son, and I wanted to try and reconnect with you both," he said.

"Alright, why now Ben?" she asked. "Look, I know I messed up so long ago, and I've been kicking myself for a very long time."

"We were so young when we got married, teenage young," he said.

"Not long after we found out we were pregnant and then everything changed." "And then soon after I went to college in California, where my parents thought I would be better off far, far, far away from Mississippi, my home, you and our baby and the rest of my family." "Until I came home and took a job in New York, and then soon we reconnected and got back together." "Yea, we did, and we were a family." "Although your family didn't approve of us."

"Yes, that's true, they didn't," he said. "My family and your family didn't approve of us." "But we still stuck together."

She smiled, "yea we did, but it wasn't easy." "You didn't make it easy."

"Most of the time I felt like a single parent because you were never home, and that's why Levy doesn't really know you, she said."

"Yes, I know this, and I take full blame for not being her for you or him, my work to all my time I admit, he said."

"Look Doreen, I know I messed up with and Levy, and I'm here because I want to make it right."

"Alright, well if you want to make it right, how about you start being honest with me right now," she said.

"Why after almost seventeen years of

marriage did you ask for a divorce?" she asked.

"Well, to be honest at the time I thought that was what I wanted but found out soon after that I had made a major mistake." "Walking away from you and Levy was a mistake that I will never forgive myself for."

"Doreen, I no doubt love my job, and always have, that's a give but I'm finding that I love my family too but, in the beginning it was a struggle to juggle work and family, and I hated myself for choosing my work over you two."

"Bottom line Doreen, I want you and Levy back in my life, and now." "I want our family back."

Doreen just sat there stunned, she didn't know what to say, of how to feel. Ben's revelation crazy, and out there. She never thought she would ever hear these words out of his mouth ever again, that he wanted to reconnect with his family again. She didn't see that one coming.

"So, let me get this straight, we divorce a couple of months ago because you were adamant about getting rid of me and Levy." "But were here not quite a week and you're here in Mississippi because you have a revelation of us being a family again."

"You know, even though we were married all those years, I felt like I was a single mom doing the very best I could for my son and myself." "I found a way to be okay with the fact that I was married but was raising my son alone, and still doing it."

Now if you'll excuse me, I'm gong to bed," she said.

"Oh yea, your room is upstairs and to the right, first door on the right," and so she stood up and headed up stairs.

He just sat there stunned, she had found a backbone to make herself known, and he respected her for that. Now, all he had to do was prove to her he was ready to be a family man. A husband and dad. He stood up and headed upstairs.

Doreen walked into her room, walked over to her desk and sat down, woke her computer up, her thoughts traveled back to hers and Ben's conversation, and what he revealed.

She had a feeling that was why he contacted her in the first place, and it made sense now.

As she thought back to when they were kids, she remembered that their parents from the being didn't approve of them, and she never understood why. Until both families found out that she and Ben were going to be parents and then all heck broke lose and all because both sets of parents couldn't get along long enough to figure out a solution, and so the Peterson's quickly sent their son away right after graduation because of their selfish ways. But as soon as he had finished college he contacted her letting her know that he was coming home for a short time and that he was taking a job in New York, and he asked her to go with him behind her families back of course, and so she told her family that she had a job waiting in New York for her and that she and her son were moving their asap, her family didn't like her decision but she didn't care, and so she followed her heart, and soon she and Ben were back together. But it take long for their families to find out but it didn't matter to them because they were together.

The more she thought about everything, the more she realized she had a lot to think about.

Ben was sitting in the guess bedroom, thinking to himself about everything he had told her. Everything was the truth. The total truth. He had nothing to lie about, especially to her.

Now he was hoping and praying that she would forgive him and take him back and give him a second chance. He vowed that this time no one or anything would get in the way of them.

CHAPTER 23

Saturday morning rolled around, an Arlene was sitting in the kitchen drinking coffee, and wondering why Ben Peterson was in her house. What could Doreen possibly want with him, after he hurt her so badly. Although if memory severed correctly she was partly to blame for them breaking up the first time.

She was in her own little world when she was interrupted by several pairs of feet coming into the kitchen.

"Hey grandma." "Hey son." "So, what's you up today?"

"I don't know yet," he said. Arlene smiled.

"Good morning mom." "Oh, good morning dear." "Did you and Ben work everything out?" she asked curiously.

Doreen looked at her son and then back at her mom, "no not yet mom." Suddenly they heard, "good morning people." They looked up, "good morning

Ben." He then looked over at Doreen with a encouraging smile.

Not long after she returned the encouraging smile back to him, and he knew at that moment they might be able to work things out.

"So, what do we have planned for today?" he asked.

"I don't know dad, you have any ideas," said Levy.

"Yea son, I do," Ben said. "Well come on family let's get this day started."

The End

9 798637 475155